LUCY TRIES SOCCER

written by
Lisa Bowes

illustrated by
James Hearne

ORCA BOOK PUBLISHERS

It's Saturday morning
with Lucy
and friends.

They're **ready** to play

on field number ten.

In her **new jersey,**
Lucy's pleased as can be.
For the **very first time,**
she'll play

**three-
on-
three!**

"Time to warm up!"
shouts the COACH of Team Blue.

His name is Nick,

and he knows what to do.

"Let's learn
and have fun,"

he says with a grin.

"We'll start with footwork—
the best place to begin."

"This is called 'tick tock.'

It helps with control.

Back and forth, side to side,
get a feel for the ball."

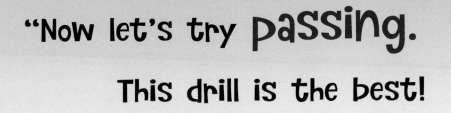

"Now let's try **passing.**

This drill is the best!

It involves **all** of you,

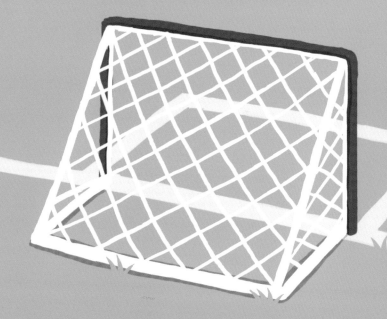

the key to success."

"Have fun and play fair.
Here they are—it's Team Red."

Lucy **dribbles** ahead
as her friends
all spread out.

A **quick pass** to Danny,
and then Danny **shouts:**

"Lucy!
Back to you.
Hurry!
Back to me."

This is "give-and-go,"
a chance for the team.

What fun,
Lucy thinks,
her heart
beating
fast.

Together with friends,
it's "footy" on grass.

Team Red must defend
Team Blue's smart attack.

Lucy **shoots** on goal.
Ava sends it back.

"Substitution, Ref!

Others need a turn.

I'm proud of you, Lucy!
You listened and learned."

Lucy **smiles** as she sees
her team **moving in.**

Claire aims at the net,
she scores!
Team Blue wins!

Let's cheer for Team Red!
And cheer for US too!

Now line up, shake hands—
it's the
right thing
to do.

Soccer or football—

no matter its name,

it's one great TEAM sport,

the world's beautiful game.

FAST FACTS!

Why is soccer called "the beautiful game"?

Soccer is called the beautiful game because of its simplistic beauty. The rules are easier to follow than in most team sports, and you can play anywhere as long as you have a ball. Soccer is the world's most popular sport; almost three billion people play the game!

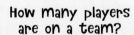

How many players are on a team?

There are eleven players on a team. Ten are either defenders, midfielders or forwards, and there is one keeper.

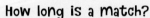

How long is a match?

A soccer game lasts ninety minutes, and the clock never stops! Not for goals, injuries or time-outs. Instead, referees add time to the end of each half to account for time lost to substitutions and goal celebrations.

Why do players shake hands after the game?

Both teams do this to show respect and good sportsmanship. *Sportsmanship* means playing fair and handling both victory and defeat with grace.

Are there soccer tournaments for kids?

The Danone Nations Cup is the world's biggest tournament for children between the ages of ten and twelve. This annual event features thirty-two participating countries and culminates in the World Final.

For my parents
—L.B.

For my three girls, Paula, Mikayla and Vicky
—J.H.

Text copyright © 2016 Lisa Bowes
Illustrations copyright © 2016 James Hearne

Library and Archives Canada Cataloguing in Publication

Bowes, Lisa, 1966–, author
Lucy tries soccer / Lisa Bowes ; illustrated by James Hearne.
(Lucy tries sports)

Issued in print and electronic formats.
ISBN 978-1-4598-1022-8 (paperback).—ISBN 978-1-4598-1023-5 (pdf).—
ISBN 978-1-4598-1024-2 (epub)

I. Hearne, James, 1972–, illustrator II. Title.
PS8603.O9758L84 2016   jc813'.6   C2015-904532-0
C2015-904533-9

First published in the United States, 2016
Library of Congress Control Number: 2015944561

Summary: In this picture book and follow-up to *Lucy Tries Short Track* and *Lucy Tries Luge*, Lucy and her friends learn a few basic soccer skills as they prepare to face Team Red.

MIX
Paper from responsible sources
FSC® C016245

Orca Book Publishers is dedicated to preserving the environment and has printed this book on Forest Stewardship Council® certified paper.

Orca Book Publishers gratefully acknowledges the support for its publishing programs provided by the following agencies: the Government of Canada through the Canada Book Fund and the Canada Council for the Arts, and the Province of British Columbia through the BC Arts Council and the Book Publishing Tax Credit.

Artwork created using hand drawings and digital coloring.

Cover artwork by James Hearne
Design by Teresa Bubela

ORCA BOOK PUBLISHERS
www.orcabook.com

Printed and bound in Canada.

19 18 17 16 • 6 5 4 3